For Florence, who is our family's Marmee
—H. V. F.

To Olga Evgrafieva
—B. I.

SIMON & SCHUSTER BOOKS FOR YOUNG READERS
An imprint of Simon & Schuster Children's Publishing Division
1230 Avenue of the Americas, New York, New York 10020
Text copyright © 2014 by Heather Vogel Frederick.
Illustrations copyright © 2014 by Bagram Ibatoulline
This work was adapted from Louisa May Alcott's *Little Women*.

For information about special discounts for bulk purchases, please contact
Simon & Schuster Special Sales at 1-866-506-1949 or business@simonandschuster.com.
The Simon & Schuster Speakers Bureau can bring authors to your live event. For more information or to book an event,
contact the Simon & Schuster Speakers Bureau at 1-866-248-3049 or visit our website at www.simonspeakers.com.
Book design by Laurent Linn
The text for this book is set in ArrusBT Std.
The illustrations for this book are rendered in Turner Acryl Gouache on paper.
Manufactured in China
0714 SCP
2 4 6 8 10 9 7 5 3 1
Library of Congress Cataloging-in-Publication Data
Frederick, Heather Vogel.
A Little women Christmas / Heather Vogel Frederick ; illustrated by Bagram Ibatoulline.—1st ed.
p. cm.
Summary: With Father away serving in the Civil War, Marmee and her girls try to have a cheery Christmas.
ISBN 978-1-4424-1359-7 (hardcover) — ISBN 978-1-4814-1833-1 (eBook)
[1. Christmas—Fiction. 2. Gifts—Fiction. 3. Sisters—Fiction. 4. Family life—New England—Fiction. 5. New England—
History—19th century—Fiction.] I. Ibatoulline, Bagram, ill. II. Alcott, Louisa May, 1832–1888. Little women. III. Title.
PZ7.F87217Li 2012
[Fic]—dc23
2011016962

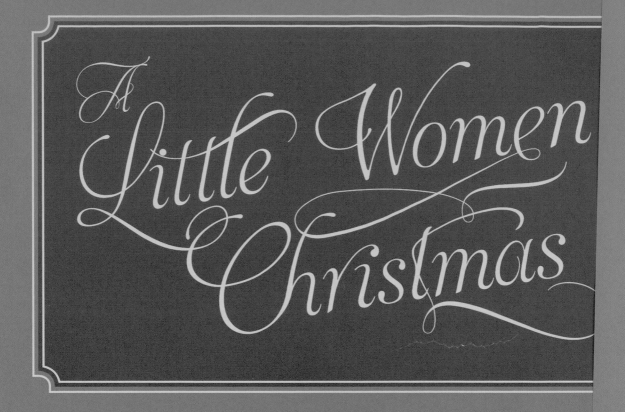

A Little Women Christmas

A Little Women Christmas

ADAPTED FROM LOUISA MAY ALCOTT'S *LITTLE WOMEN*

HEATHER VOGEL
FREDERICK

Illustrated by BAGRAM
IBATOULLINE

Simon & Schuster Books for Young Readers

NEW YORK   LONDON   TORONTO   SYDNEY   NEW DELHI

"Hush!" whispered Jo. "They'll hear us!"

Stifling their laughter, the pair put the finishing touches on their creation and stepped back to admire their handiwork.

"It's perfect," said Laurie—Theodore Laurence officially, but Laurie to his friends. "A perfect present for Beth."

Jo glanced toward the house where her mother and sisters were gathered inside the parlor. She smiled. This Christmas would be different for her family. This year there would be presents. She and Laurie were seeing to that. Christmas just wasn't Christmas without presents.

The two friends bid each other good night and Laurie ducked through the hedge to his home next door. Jo paused to peek in the window.

A fire crackled cheerfully on the hearth. Beside it, her mother and Meg were knitting socks for faraway soldiers. Amy was bent over her sketchbook. Only Beth's hands were still. Thin and pale from her most recent illness, she leaned quietly against her mother's knee. A shadow passed across Jo's face as her gaze fell on Father's empty chair.

It had been empty for a very long time.

More than a year had passed since Mr. March had gone off to war, leaving the five of them behind. He was a chaplain for the Union army, ministering to a flock of blue-uniformed soldiers. This Christmas, though, instead of camped in a tent on a frozen battlefield, he was in a hospital in Washington, DC. Like Beth, Mr. March had been gravely ill.

Jo lifted her face heavenward. The night air was cold and clear, the sky bright with stars. Were they shining on Father, too?

She shivered and pulled the hood of her cloak over her close-cropped hair. She had sold the rest for money to help Father. It was the only gift she could think to give him.

Christmas morning brought sunshine, along with smiles from Beth as Marmee—the March girls' pet name for their mother—wrapped her in a new red shawl.

"There are more presents, too!" said Jo, sweeping Beth up in her arms and carrying her downstairs to the window.

Beth's eyes widened as she spied the surprise. "Oh!" she cried in delight. "A snow maiden!"

And indeed it was, with a crown of holly upon her wintry head. One icy hand held a basket of fruit and flowers, the other a sheaf of new piano music. Draped around her chilly shoulders was a colorful knitted blanket, and from her silent lips fluttered a pink paper streamer that bore a Christmas carol:

God bless you, dear Queen Bess!
May nothing you dismay,
But health and peace and happiness
Be yours this Christmas Day.

Beth was not the only one to receive a present. For Amy, the artist in the family, there was a framed picture, and for Jo, who meant to be a writer someday, a book, of course. Thanks to Laurie's grandfather, Meg had a new silk dress—her first!

And for Marmee? Mrs. March needed no gift
but the knowledge that her youngest daughter was
well and her husband safe, but she was given one
anyway—a lovely brooch the girls had made by
intertwining locks of their hair.

"I'm so full of happiness that, if Father were only here, I couldn't hold one drop more," said Beth, and her sisters quite agreed.

"We have much to be thankful for, girls," Marmee reminded them gently. "Your father may not be with us today, but he will be again and that's more than many a family can say."

Now and then in this workaday
world delightful things do happen,
for some time later the final drop to
their cup of happiness was added
when the parlor door flew open
and Laurie poked his head in.

"Here's another present for the
March family!" he cried, stepping
aside to reveal a tall figure
standing behind him.

Though he was wrapped to the eyes in a greatcoat and muffler, his family knew him in an instant.

Father was home!

Never was there such a Christmas dinner as they had that day, with a fat turkey and plum pudding and stories and songs.

"I know it's been a rough road for you to travel," Mr. March told his wife and daughters, lifting his glass in a toast. "But you have got on bravely."

Mrs. March smiled. "We did as we've always done—hoped and kept busy."

After dinner, Mr. March settled into the chair by the fireside that had been empty for so long. He looked with fatherly satisfaction at the four young faces gathered around him, and smiled as he took his eldest daughter's hand.

"Here's industrious Meg, who has helped keep home happy, and Amy"—he reached out to stroke her shining hair—"whose talent lies in making life beautiful to herself and others." Hugging Beth close, he whispered, "And I've got you safe, my Beth, and will keep you so, please God."

"What about Jo?" Beth pleaded. "Please say something nice, for she has tried so hard and been so very, very good."

Mr. March laughed. "I don't know if the shearing has sobered our black sheep, and I rather miss my wild girl, but if I get a strong, helpful, tenderhearted woman in her place, I am quite satisfied."

Marmee's eyes shone with quiet joy as her husband gazed around the loving circle and added, "I am prouder than ever of all my little women."

The March family's full hearts overflowed, and Beth sighed in contentment. "We have Father and Mother and each other," she said. "That's the very best present of all."